The Great Gran Plan

For my Mum
and for my late, great, Aussie grandmother,
Gwen 'Mate' Hearnshaw - E.W.

In memory of Evelyn and Wyn,
my two lovely grandmas - S.L.

First published 2017 by Macmillan Children's Books,
an imprint of Pan Macmillan, 20 New Wharf Road, London N1 9RR.
Associated companies throughout the world.
www.panmacmillan.com

ISBN: 978-1-4472-5478-2 (HB)
ISBN:978-1-4472-5479-9 (PB)

1 3 5 7 9 8 6 4 2

Printed in China

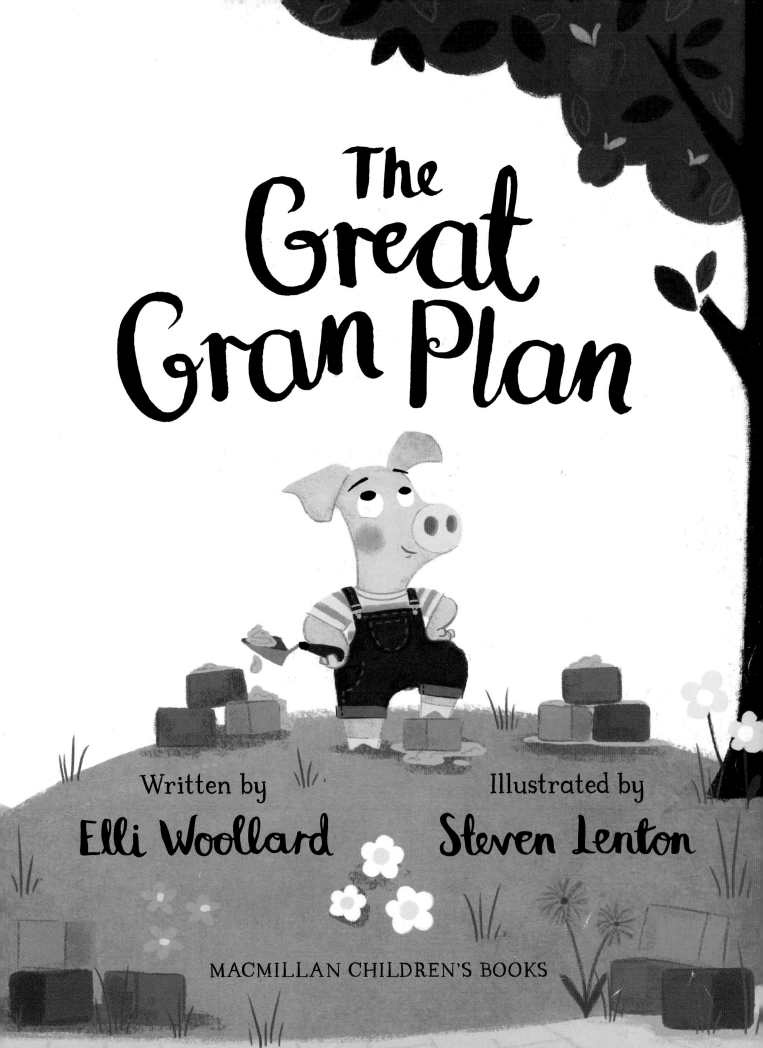

The Great Gran Plan

Written by
Elli Woollard

Illustrated by
Steven Lenton

MACMILLAN CHILDREN'S BOOKS

The pig had a house in the Wild Wild Wood.
It was safe, it was strong, it was snug, it was good!

So when the bad wolf started howling and prowling
and skulking and scowling and grizzling and growling,

The pig said, "Old wolf, you can blow till you're blue!
But you'll not break my house down, whatever you do."

The wolf simply glared, then slunk slowly away.
But there, on the pathway, the very next day,
the pig found a note that said . . .

TOP SECRET PLOT

1. ~~Eat the Three Little Pigs~~

2. Gobble Red Riding Hood's gran nice and hot!

"No!" cried the pig. "Oh my trusty old trotter!
That stinky old fleabag, that wily old rotter!
And he leapt to the wheel of his rusty old van,
crying, "Pig to the rescue,

SAVE THAT GRAN!"

GIANT! SALE!

"I'll snatch him, I'll catch him,
That wolf won't escape!
But first what I need is a Superpig cape."

Apple Stall

WIZARD WEAR

Staffs Wanted

Wanda's Wands

So he
dashed
through the
town till he
came to a stall.
They hadn't a cape . . .

. . . but they gave him a shawl.

Then he leapt to the wheel of his rusty old van,
crying, "Pig to the rescue,

SAVE THAT GRAN!"

"Now I'll have to be sneaky, I might have to spy.
Binoculars! Yes! I should give them a try."

JUST
RIGHTS

OPEN

P1G E

So he dashed to the shop, and there weren't any there!

But he did find some rather fine specs (the last pair).

Then he leapt to the wheel of his rusty old van,
crying, "Pig to the rescue,

SAVE THAT GRAN!"

"I'll swoop on that wolfie, I'll hoop him, I hope.
But now what I need is some lovely strong rope."
So he dashed to the city; the shops were so full!

Emporium of New Clothes

ROPE-UNZEL'S

Peep's BO-tique

OPEN ALL KNIGHT

And the rope was sold out . . .

. . . but he did find some wool.

WOOL
SALE

BAARB

LUCKY
SHEEP
DIP

Then he ran to the wheel of his rusty old van,
crying, "Pig to the rescue,

SAVE
THAT
GRAN!"

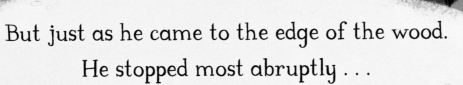

But just as he came to the edge of the wood.

He stopped most abruptly . . .

. . . as there the wolf stood!

"Red Riding Hood's granny? Well how do you do?
Strangely enough, I've been searching for you.
Although, I admit that it's quite a surprise!
You've got such a strange nose and such small piggy eyes."

"Gran?" thought the pig, and he took a long look . . .

Then he quivered and quaked and he shivered and shook.

The wolf eyed him up and snarled, "Mmm, nice and plump!
Not old and not chewy - just look at that rump!
You'd taste rather rare in a butty, I bet."
And he lunged at the pig, but then . . .

. . . down came a net!

And there, in the wood, was Red Riding Hood's gran,
who cried, "Think we can't catch you?

YOU BET THAT WE CAN!"

"You wicked old wolf, you may huff, you may puff,
but I'm telling you now, I have had quite ENOUGH!"

Then she tied up the wolf from his nose to his tail.
And together they took him and dropped him in jail.

"Thanks!" cried the pig, but the gran said, "Thank *you!*
That wolf would have minced me for grey granny stew!"

And linking together they danced out a jig.
The wolf-busting gran and the clever young pig.

"Yes!" They both said,
"We're an excellent team!"

And the wolf never came there again . . .

. . . it would seem.

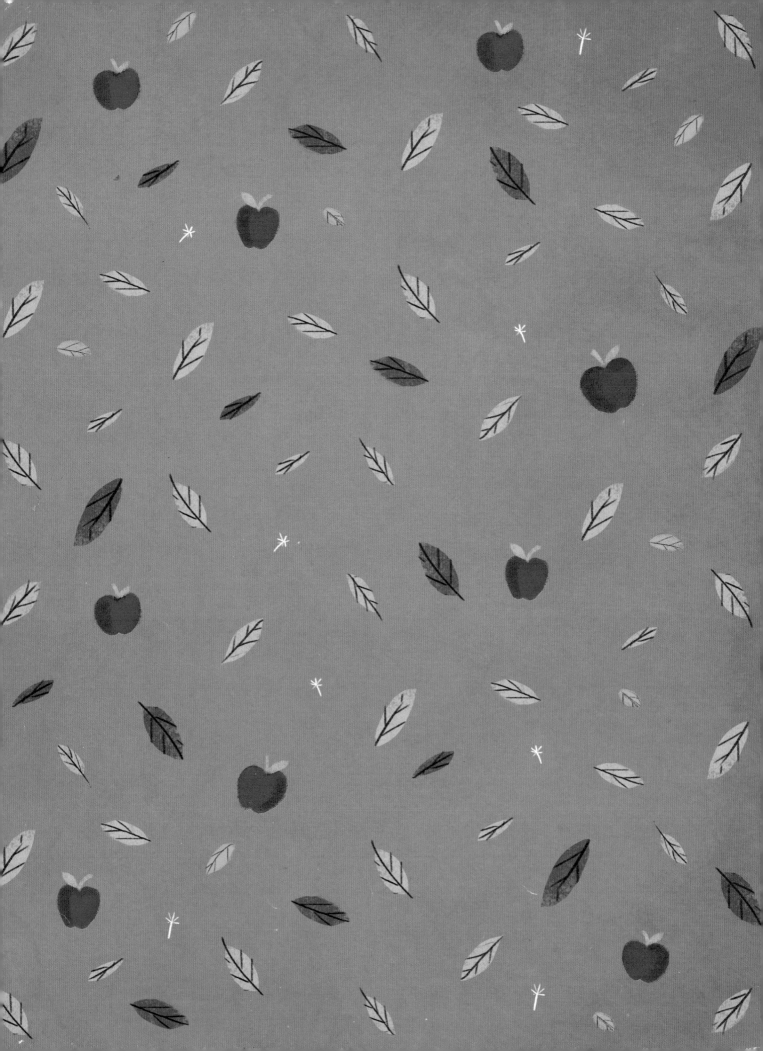